Debi Gliori

Flora's Blanket

ORCHARD BOOKS

Flora couldn't sleep.

With lots of love to Lindsey Fraser
(who really knows the true worth
of a good blanket...)

ORCHARD BOOKS
96 Leonard Street, London EC2A 4XD
Orchard Books Australia
Unit 31/56 O'Riordan St, Alexandria NSW 2015
First published in Great Britain in 2001
ISBN 1 84121 555 4
A CIP catalogue record for this book is available from the British Library
3 5 7 9 10 8 6 4 2
Printed in Dubai

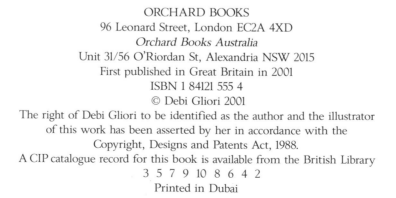

"Poor Flora, what's wrong?"
said her Dad. "Sore tummy?"

"No," said Flora.

"Oh Flora," said her Mum.
"Do your ears hurt?"

"No," said Flora.

"Whatever is the matter, Flora?" said her brothers and sisters.

"Why won't you sleep?"

"No blanket," said Flora.

"Have mine," offered Norah.

"Or mine," said Cora.

"No," said Flora.

"Here, take ours,"
said Sam, Tom and Max.

"No," said Flora.
"Want mine."

"Where is your blanket, Flora?" sighed her Mum.

"Don't know," muttered Flora.

"Let's go find it," groaned her Dad.

So they looked in the
living room.
"No," said Flora.

And the kitchen.
"No," said
Flora.

And the bathroom.
"No," said Flora.

Then they tried outside.
The sandpit?

The climbing tree?

The vegetable patch?

"No! NO! NO!"
yelled Flora.

Then they looked
in odd places.
The fridge?

"No",
sighed
Flora.

The greenhouse?

"No," yawned Flora.

The cellar?
"Flora?"
said her Dad.

But Flora was
nearly asleep.

Flora's Mum and Dad
tucked her up in
their bed.

Flora's Mum and Dad
went to bed too.

"What's this lump under my pillow?" said Flora's Dad.

It can't be Flora's teddy.

It can't be Flora's book.

It must be...

Flora's blanket!

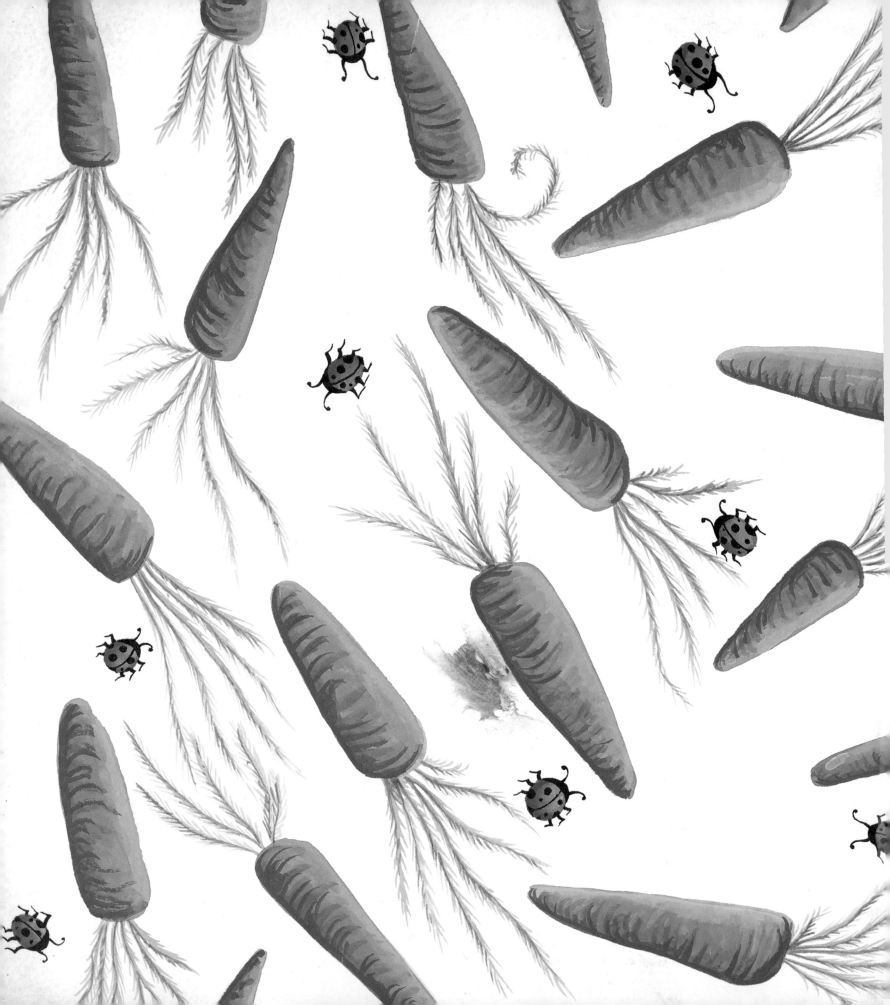